. . . for parents and teachers

Death — a difficult topic for all of us — is especially
hard to discuss with children. *Why Did Grandma Die?*
encourages very young people to talk about their normal
fears and anxieties about dying, with their parents, teachers,
and other professionals.

This book presents the major concepts that death is a
natural part of life, and that death is not temporary, as
many young children tend to believe. Also introduced are
some common funeral customs and exposure to appropriate
ways of grieving. There is room for parents to fill in their
own religious, social, and cultural values.

Most importantly, this book promotes children's
awareness of the feelings, both positive and negative, that
they have for others, and the sharing of those feelings with
loved ones.

The ideal time to educate is *before* a personal crisis arises
that makes allaying fears and correcting misconceptions a
necessity — at the very time when parents may themselves
be least able to cope. Furthermore, since death is a common
theme that children are exposed to on television, it is
essential that education about death not be left to chance.

There is no age, therefore, at which *Why Did Grandma
Die?* would be inappropriate to start that education.

GLORIA J. LEWIS, Ph.D.
ASSOCIATE PROFESSOR
DEPARTMENT OF GUIDANCE AND
   COUNSELING
LOYOLA UNIVERSITY OF CHICAGO

Library of Congress Number: 79-23892

1 2 3 4 5 6 7 8 9 0 84 83 82 81 80

Printed in the United States of America.

Library of Congress Cataloging in Publication Data

Madler, Trudy.
  Why did grandma die?

  SUMMARY: When her grandmother dies, Heidi tries to
deal with her feelings of grief and loss and comes to
accept death as part of the life cycle by attending
the funeral and talking to others about her feelings.
  [1. Death — Fiction] I. Connelly, Gwen. II. Title.
PZ7.M2656Wh   [Fic]   79-23892
ISBN 0-8172-1354-6 lib. bdg.

WHY DID GRANDMA DIE?

by *Trudy Madler*

illustrated by Gwen Connelly

introduction by Gloria J. Lewis, Ph.D.

RAINTREE CHILDRENS BOOKS
Milwaukee • Toronto • Melbourne • London

"I'm home!" shouted Heidi.

She slammed the front door behind her and ran into the living room.

All day long Heidi had been waiting for this minute. Today was the day her grandmother was taking her to the park for a pony ride. Heidi loved horses, and so did her grandmother.

The curtains were drawn in the living room. At first Heidi couldn't see anything.

Then she saw her little brother, Bobby, still in his pajamas. And there, stretched out on the sofa, was her grandmother.

"Grandma, why aren't you ready?" asked Heidi. "You didn't forget about the pony ride, did you?"

Her grandmother sat up a little. "How could I forget a thing like that?" she said. "I'm just tired, that's all. I've been resting."

Heidi frowned.

"I'm sorry, Heidi. We'll go tomorrow, I promise. You *know* I'm just as excited about going as you are."

Heidi nodded and smiled.

"Come on into the kitchen with me," said her grandmother. "Your mother and father will be home soon. I have to get supper started. You sit down and tell me what happened in school today. I want to hear everything."

Heidi and her grandmother moved Bobby's playpen into the kitchen. Then her grandmother made up a big batch of clay and showed Heidi how to make a horse out of the clay. That was one of the things Heidi loved most about her grandmother — she was always making such beautiful things.

Heidi sat at the kitchen table while her grandmother worked near the stove. Heidi was busy working with the clay and chattering. She didn't notice that her grandmother wasn't answering Heidi very often.

9

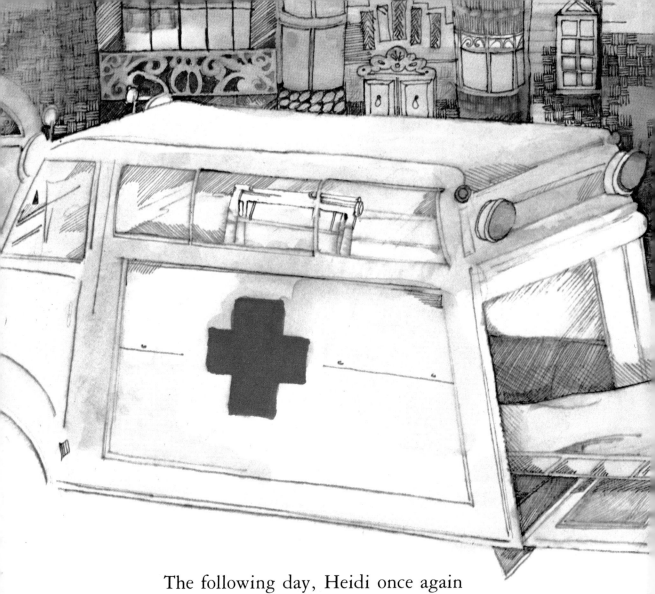

The following day, Heidi once again
raced home from school.

She didn't know what to think when she
saw a white truck parked in front of her
building. Red lights flashed. Two men
were lifting someone into the truck.

It was her grandmother.

Heidi's mother stood near the truck.
Heidi ran to her.

"Where is Grandma going?" she cried.
"And why are you home from work?
What's going on?"

Heidi's mother held her close.
"Grandma is very sick. She's going to the
hospital. I'm going along with her, and
Dad is meeting us there."

"I'll come too," Heidi said.

"No, it would be better if you stayed
home with Bobby. Mrs. Kane will look
after you till we get back."

Her mother gave her a kiss and got
into the truck.

Mrs. Kane was the neighbor who lived across the hall. She was already cooking supper when Heidi came into the apartment.

"Have some of my cookies," said Mrs. Kane. "Supper won't be ready for a while."

"My grandma says cookies are bad for your teeth," Heidi said. She didn't mean to sound rude, but she was so worried about her grandmother that she could hardly think straight.

"These cookies have lots of good things in them," said Mrs. Kane. "I do love to bake. My own grandchildren live far away, so I thought I'd bake some for you."

Heidi didn't answer.

That night, she fell asleep before her parents came home. When she woke up the following morning, her mother was sitting on her bed.

"I have some sad news," she said. "Grandma won't be coming home. She died last night."

"Died?" Heidi whispered. "Why? Why did Grandma die?"

"Well, Grandma was very old."

"You mean people die just because they're old?"

"Sometimes," said her mother. "A person's heart is always beating. After many years it wears down. That's what happened to Grandma. Many old people are ready to die. They know that death is a natural part of life. Your grandma had a long and good life."

"I — I don't know," Heidi said. "I think you and Dad could have done something . . . something that would have saved her."

Her mother looked very tired. "Everyone tried their best," she said softly.

That day Heidi stayed home from
school. Her parents stayed home from
work too.

No one ate much at breakfast.

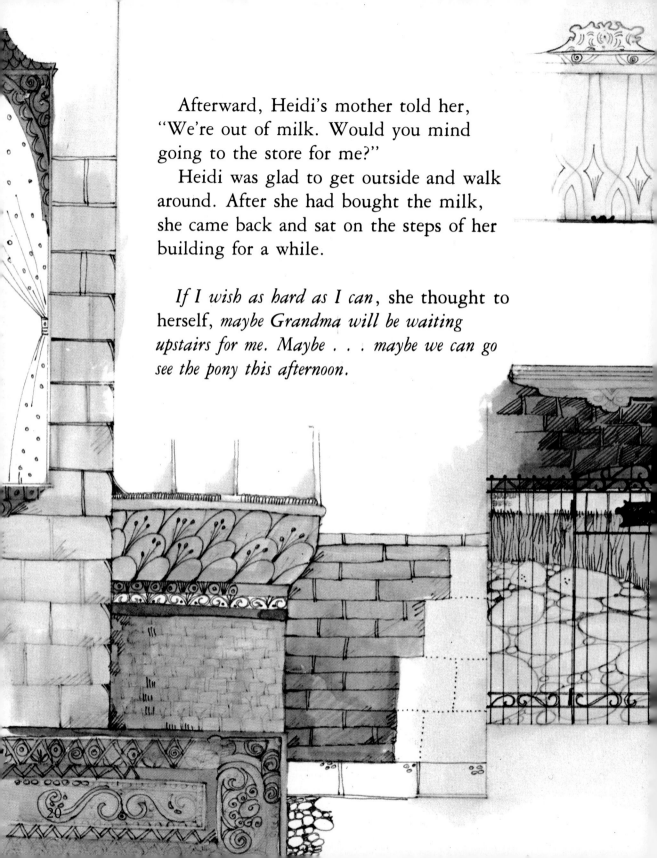

Afterward, Heidi's mother told her, "We're out of milk. Would you mind going to the store for me?"

Heidi was glad to get outside and walk around. After she had bought the milk, she came back and sat on the steps of her building for a while.

If I wish as hard as I can, she thought to herself, *maybe Grandma will be waiting upstairs for me. Maybe . . . maybe we can go see the pony this afternoon.*

20

When she got up to the apartment, the only people in the kitchen besides her parents were her Uncle Joe and Aunt Connie. Heidi liked them both, but today the only person she wanted was her grandmother.

Without a word, she ran into her bedroom and started crying.

A few minutes later, her father came into the room. His eyes were red too.

"It's okay to cry," he said. "We all miss Grandma, and crying is a good way of showing it."

"Oh, Dad, I was wishing so hard that she was here again."

"I know," he said. "But when people die, nothing can bring them back."

Suddenly Heidi stood up. "But I didn't even say good-bye!"

"Grandma knew how much you loved her. That's what matters most."

It seemed like half the city was there for the funeral. Heidi couldn't believe how many friends and relatives her grandmother had had. Having all those people there to share her sadness made Heidi feel a little better.

Some of the people made speeches, which Heidi had a hard time paying attention to. Then everyone took a turn going up to the place where the body of Heidi's grandmother was, to show their love and respect.

Heidi stared at her grandmother's body for a moment. *Good-bye*, she said silently. *I love you.*

24

Many of the people came back to Heidi's apartment after the funeral.

Heidi was standing by the window, looking at her grandmother's flower box, when Mrs. Kane came up behind her.

"I've been talking to your parents," said Mrs. Kane. "While they're at work, I'm going to take care of you and Bobby."

"The only one I want to take care of me is my grandma," Heidi said without thinking.

Mrs. Kane looked down. "Why don't you think it over?" she said, then turned away.

Heidi's father walked over and put his arm around her. "Come on," he said. "Let's take a walk."

They went to the park. They found an empty bench and watched children riding ponies and playing ball.

"If Grandma's heart wore out," Heidi said slowly, "does that mean my heart is going to wear out too?"

"In time everyone dies," said her father. "But they always leave something behind."

"You mean like Grandma left her flower box?"

"That too," her father said. "But what I meant was that it's the things you remember that stay with you."

"I remember lots of things about Grandma. She liked horses. And she was always showing me how to make clay animals."

"And maybe someday you'll show someone else. That's a part of Grandma that you'll always have with you."

Heidi was quiet. Then she took her father's hand. "Can we go back now? I have to talk to Mrs. Kane."

"Why?"

"She must hate me. I told her I only wanted Grandma to take care of me."

"If you tell her you're sorry, she'll understand."

They walked down the street together. Heidi stopped in front of their building.

"Look at Grandma's flowers — they're all dry," she said. "After I talk to Mrs. Kane, I'd better give them some water."

"Want some help?" her father asked.

Heidi smiled. "Sure!"